tWS

D0262481

Please return/renew this item by the last date shown

Beowulf
and
Grendel

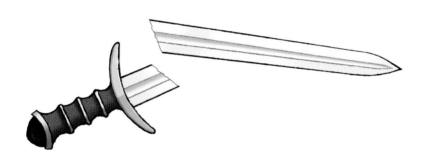

by Martin Waddell and Graham Howells

W
FRANKLIN WATTS
LONDON•SYDNEY

First published in 2009 by
Franklin Watts
338 Euston Road
London
NW1 3BH

Franklin Watts Australia
Level 17/207 Kent Street
Sydney
NSW 2000

Text © Martin Waddell 2009
Illustrations © Graham Howells 2009

A CIP catalogue record for this book is available
from the British Library.

ISBN 978 0 7496 8551 5 (hbk)
ISBN 978 0 7496 8563 8 (pbk)

Series Editor: Jackie Hamley
Series Advisor: Dr Barrie Wade
Series Designer: Peter Scoulding

Printed in China

Franklin Watts is a division of
Hachette Children's Books,
an Hachette UK company
www.hachette.co.uk

The Great Hall of King Hrothgar
the Dane rang with music
and laughter.

Nearby in a dark, stinking swamp, something stirred as night fell. The monster Grendel hated all men because they were not like him. They laughed and made music. He wanted only to kill and destroy.

Grendel's eyes burned red
and his heart filled with rage.

Full of hatred, he crawled
from the swamp.

CRASH!

One blow of his claw smashed
the door to pieces.

Men screamed as Grendel
attacked. Their swords broke
against his tough skin.

Grendel filled a huge, dragon-skin
bag with human flesh.

Blood dripped from the bag as he
dragged it back to his lair.

The monster came back night after night. He killed again ...

... and again ...

... and again.

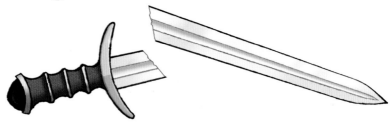

Stories of the evil Grendel reached the great warrior Beowulf.

Beowulf had fought many monsters.

"Grendel kills men, women and children," everyone told him. "Hrothgar's people are in despair."

"Then I shall sail with my men to save them," Beowulf vowed. "We'll leave tonight."

"No one can fight Grendel!" King Hrothgar told Beowulf. "The force of evil protects him. Swords and armour are no use against him."

"I will fight as he fights, with neither sword nor armour," said Beowulf. "Then you'll die," sighed Hrothgar. "Good always defeats evil," Beowulf said, "and my soul is good."

That night, Beowulf and his followers waited in Hrothgar's Great Hall. Sure enough, Grendel came slithering from the swamp.

The door of the Great Hall
was bound by metal bars, but
Grendel's huge claws snapped
them like twigs.

Beowulf faced the monster.
As Grendel lifted his immense
claws to strike, Beowulf grabbed
him by the wrist. The warrior's
iron grip pressed deep into
the monster's tough skin.

Grendel screamed in pain, but
he could not escape the strange
power of the warrior's grip.

Grendel struggled wildly, trying to bite off Beowulf's head, his arms, his legs, but somehow Beowulf held on. Then ...

ARGH! Grendel tore free, leaving his arm behind him.

The monster fled, dripping blood
from his terrible wound.

Beowulf followed him to the muddy swamp where the water boiled blood red as the monster died.

Beowulf stuck Grendel's head on a spear and took it to King Hrothgar.

The good in Beowulf had given him the strength to beat the evil Grendel.

As his ship sailed away, music and laughter rang round Hrothgar's Great Hall once more.

Puzzle 1

Put these pictures in the correct order.
Which event do you think is most important?
Now try writing the story in your own words!

Puzzle 2

1. How can I save my people?

2. I will kill every one of them.

3. Evil will never win.

4. Our weapons cannot hurt him.

5. I hate ...

6. Only goodness will beat him.

Choose the correct speech bubbles for each character. Can you think of any others? Turn over to find the answers.

Answers

Puzzle 1

The correct order is: 1d, 2b, 3a, 4f, 5e, 6c

Puzzle 2

Beowulf: 3, 6

Grendel: 2, 5

King Hrothgar: 1, 4

Look out for more Hopscotch Adventures:

Aladdin and the Lamp
ISBN 978 0 7496 6692 7

Blackbeard the Pirate
ISBN 978 0 7496 6690 3

George and the Dragon
ISBN 978 0 7496 6691 0

Jack the Giant-Killer
ISBN 978 0 7496 6693 4

Beowulf and Grendel
ISBN 978 0 7496 8551 5*
ISBN 978 0 7496 8563 8

Agnes and the Giant
ISBN 978 0 7496 8552 2*
ISBN 978 0 7496 8564 5

The Dragon and the Pudding
ISBN 978 0 7496 8549 2*
ISBN 978 0 7496 8561 4

Finn MacCool and the Giant's Causeway
ISBN 978 0 7496 8550 8*
ISBN 978 0 7496 8562 1

TALES OF KING ARTHUR

1. The Sword in the Stone
ISBN 978 0 7496 6694 1

2. Arthur the King
ISBN 978 0 7496 6695 8

3. The Round Table
ISBN 978 0 7496 6697 2

4. Sir Lancelot and the Ice Castle
ISBN 978 0 7496 6698 9

5. Sir Gawain and the Green Knight
ISBN 978 0 7496 8557 7*
ISBN 978 0 7496 8569 0

6. Sir Galahad and the Holy Grail
ISBN 978 0 7496 8558 4*
ISBN 978 0 7496 8570 6

TALES OF ROBIN HOOD

Robin and the Knight
ISBN 978 0 7496 6699 6

Robin and the Monk
ISBN 978 0 7496 6700 9

Robin and the Silver Arrow
ISBN 978 0 7496 6703 0

Robin and the Friar
ISBN 978 0 7496 6702 3

Robin and the Butcher
ISBN 978 0 7496 8555 3*
ISBN 978 0 7496 8568 3

Robin and Maid Marian
ISBN 978 0 7496 8556 0*
ISBN 978 0 7496 8567 6

For more Hopscotch books go to:
www.franklinwatts.co.uk

* hardback   **Tales of Sinbad the Sailor also available!**